Melinda's No's Cold

written by Gail Chislett
art by Hélène Desputeaux

Annick Press Ltd., Toronto,
Canada

Melinda favoured lavender lace.
Pink bows were more to Cynthia's taste.
They wore socks of snow-white,
    pulled up to the knee
And when they sat down,
    they sat carefully.
They loved to play house,
    especially tea party.
Their dolls became real
and joined in quite smartly.
The girls spoke politely,
    their manners were great,
They never picked their noses
    or licked the plate.
Those two were so perfect,
    it would give you a chill,
They were strictly unnatural;
    heck, they'd never been ill.

The sun was barely up one morning when a gigantic sneeze shook the house of Melinda and Cynthia Sweeting. Mrs. Sweeting rushed to Melinda's bedroom to find her snorting and sneezing into her pillow, screaming, "NO, NO, NO, NO."
She was not feeling well!

Mrs. Sweeting knew an emergency when she saw one. Wasting no time, she summoned the doctor.

By the time the doctor had opened his big black bag, the "*NO*'s" coming from Melinda were deafening.

"Oh, doctor, whatever's the matter with Melinda?"

"We'll know in a minute," he said as he drew a long rod from his bag. "This is a *NO*meter. It'll tell us how ill she is."

"ILL!" Her eyes bugged out. "But she's never been sick a day in her life. We are never unwell in this family." She looked down her nose at him.

It was a struggle to get the *NO*meter into Melinda's mouth.

Nervously, they watched the red line rise higher and higher. A 10-*NO*. A 20-*NO*. A 30-*NO*. A 40-*NO*. A 50-*NO*.

They looked at each other, horrified—A 60-*NO*.

Suddenly, Melinda gave a twitch and roared, "NOOO!!!"
The *NO*meter shot across the room.
The doctor picked it up, looked at it, and shook his head sadly.
"It's a 100-*NO*. The poor girl has got a bad *NO*'s cold."

Her mother gasped, "Doctor, what can we do?"

Smiling, he produced a bottle of pills from his bag.

"She'll feel better with this in her belly," he promised, holding up a large lavender tablet.

"NO!" Melinda almost deafened the doctor when he tried to fit the pill into her belly-button.

"Make her comfortable," he called back as he scurried out the door. "But I'm afraid she won't take it lying down."

Melinda's mother brought her adorable little biscuits and hot milk.

"NO," shrieked Melinda, and blew them across the room.

In the corner, Cynthia and the dolls huddled quietly and watched.

Later, Melinda's mother brought jam cookies and candies, a chocolate cake, a teddy bear, and a new lavender lace nightie.

"I'm not hungry, and my hand is all shaky," said Melinda, her fingers trembling about the cake. "I seem to be about to..."

"Oh goodness. Oh no. Stand back. Clear the room," cried Mrs. Sweeting. "I think she's going to throw up!"

She was right.

Suddenly, Melinda began pitching and tossing her food, dolls, the pillow— just about everything—into the air.

"Boy," said Cynthia as she scurried out of range, "She must be feeling very bad!"

By bedtime Melinda was exhausted. She had spent the entire day blowing her *NO*'s and throwing up everything within reach.

"Whatever will we do if it goes right into her chest during the night?" Mrs. Sweeting asked frantically.

"NO!" roared Melinda fiercely. "NOT INTO MY CHEST!"

Early the next morning when Cynthia
ventured into her room, Melinda was cool-
cheeked, well-behaved, and smiling.

"Did it go into your chest?" inquired
Cynthia cautiously.

With a sly smile, Melinda said,
"Look and see."

Cynthia carefully eased up the lid of Melinda's toy chest and peered in. It was too jumbled inside to see much. Leaning over, she began to investigate.

Abruptly, Cynthia reared back and the lid fell shut. She gave a sneeze that rustled the curtains.

"NO!" yelled Cynthia.

"Oh too bad, now you've caught it," said Melinda.

When Mrs. Sweeting came in with the breakfast tray, she found Cynthia blowing her *NO*'s at the top of her voice. Melinda's bed was empty.

"Mommy, I think I've got the flew, now," called Melinda as she flapped past in her nightie.

Mrs. Sweeting collapsed onto the bed.

Melinda spent the entire day swooping about the house, while Cynthia writhed in bed roaring, "NOOO!!!" even louder than her sister had.

Towards evening, things were beginning to look better. As Melinda settled for a rest on the top of Cynthia's bedroom door, she could tell that Cynthia was improving. She had stopped blowing her *NO*'s and ripping the pink bows off all her clothes, but she was hovering about a meter above the bed.

"Getting the flew, now, I see," said Melinda.

"I'm fine now," exclaimed Cynthia defiantly as she forced herself back into bed.

Neither girl got much sleep that night. They were up many times with the flew.

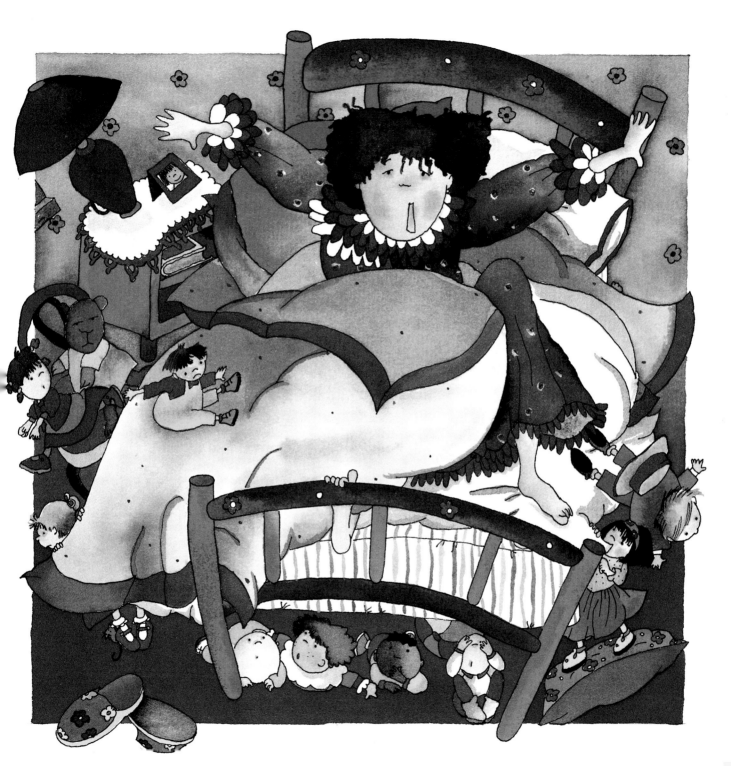

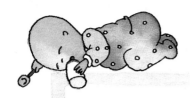

Mrs. Sweeting was so pleased when things got back to normal. It was such a relief to see Melinda and Cynthia once more having a civilized tea party. She hoped they would never, ever, ever, EVER be ill again.

"I wonder if we'll ever get sick again," said Cynthia as she poured for the dolls.

"Why, who can tell," Melinda said as she politely passed the biscuits. "Your pink bows do look lovely today, Cynthia."

"Thank you, Melinda. How your lavender lace becomes you."

"Melinda," said Cynthia as she gently dabbed her lips clean, "I hear that if you yell and yell, you get a little horse."

"Horse? A little horse? Oh, Cynthia," cried Melinda with delight, "Let's go right out and try it!"

Melinda favoured lavender lace.
Pink bows were more to Cynthia's taste.
They wore socks of snow-white,
pulled up to the knee
And when they sat down,
they sat carefully.
They loved to play house,
especially tea party.
Their dolls became real
and joined in quite smartly.
The girls spoke politely,
their manners were great,
They rarely picked their noses
or licked the plate.
Sometimes they refused to behave
as they should,
They'd stir up some mischief—
life's dull when you're good.

To Jessica, Elizabeth, and Stefanie — G.C.
To Rosalie — H.D.

Graphic design and realization by Michel Aubin

Annick Press gratefully acknowledges
the support of The Canada Council and
The Ontario Arts Council

Canadian Cataloguing in Publication Data

Chislett, Gail
    Melinda's no's cold

    ISBN 1-55037-196-7 (bound) ISBN 1-55037-198-3 (pbk.)

    I. Desputeaux, Hélène.   II. Title.

    PS8555.H5M4 1991   jC813'.54   C91-093935-7
    PZ7.C48Me 1991

Distributed in Canada and the USA by:
Firefly Books Ltd.
250 Sparks Avenue
Willowdale, Ontario
M2H 2S4 Canada

This book is printed on acid free paper

printed and bound in Canada by
D.W. Friesen & Sons Ltd.